Dear Parents and Teachers,

In an easy-reader format, **My Readers** introduce classic stories to children who are learning to read. Favorite characters and time-tested tales are the basis for **My Readers**, which are available in three levels:

1 **Level One** is for the emergent reader and features repetitive language and word clues in the illustrations.

2 **Level Two** is for more advanced readers who still need support saying and understanding some words. Stories are longer with word clues in the illustrations.

3 **Level Three** is for independent, fluent readers who enjoy working out occasional unfamiliar words. The stories are longer and divided into chapters.

Encourage children to select books based on interests, not reading levels. Read aloud with children, showing them how to use the illustrations for clues. With adult guidance and rereading, children will eventually read the desired book on their own.

Here are some ways you might want to use this book with children:

- Talk about the title and the cover illustrations. Encourage the child to use these to predict what the story is about.
- Discuss the interior illustrations and try to piece together a story based on the pictures. Does the child want to change or adjust his first prediction?
- After children reread a story, suggest they retell or act out a favorite part.

My Readers will not only help children become readers, they will serve as an introduction to some of the finest classic children's books available today.

—LAURA ROBB
Educator and Reading Consultant

For activities and reading tips, visit myreadersonline.com.

SQUARE
FISH

An Imprint of Macmillan Children's Publishing Group

Printed in China by Toppan Leefung Printing Ltd., Dongguan City, Guangdong Province.
For information, address Square Fish, 175 Fifth Avenue, New York, NY 10010.

Square Fish books may be purchased for business or promotional use. For information on bulk purchases,
please contact the Macmillan Corporate and Premium Sales Department at (800) 221-7945 x5442
or by e-mail at specialmarkets@macmillan.com

Library of Congress Cataloging-in-Publication Data Available

ISBN 978-1-250-04447-1 (hardcover)
1 3 5 7 9 10 8 6 4 2
ISBN 978-1-250-04448-8 (paperback)
1 3 5 7 9 10 8 6 4 2

Book design by Patrick Collins/Véronique Lefèvre Sweet

Square Fish logo designed by Filomena Tuosto

Previously published in similar form in *The Cat on the Mat Is Flat*
by Feiwel and Friends, an imprint of Macmillan.

First MY READERS Edition: 2014

myreadersonline.com
mackids.com

This is a Level 2 book

Lexile 470L

Ed and Ted and Ted's Dog Fred

Andy Griffiths

Illustrated by
Terry Denton

SQUARE
FISH

Macmillan Children's Publishing Group
New York

There was a man.

His name was Ed.

Ed lived in a shed

with his friend Ted.

Ted had a dog.

His name was Fred.

Fred liked Ted,

but he didn't like Ed.

One morning,

Fred jumped

on Ed's bed.

"Fred, get off my bed!"

said Ed.

Fred just barked

and bit Ed's head.

"I'm fed up

with Fred," said Ed.

"I'm leaving this shed."

Ed jumped in his car,

which was red.

"Ed!" called Ted.

"Come back to the shed!"

But Ed just shook his head.

Away he sped.

Ted jumped in his car,

which was also red.

But Ted's car wouldn't start.

The battery was dead.

Ted's face went red.

"Bother!" he said.

"I'll have to take the sled, instead."

Ted hitched up Fred

to the front of the sled

(which, by the way,

was also red)

and away

from the shed

sped Fred and Ted.

Ted and Fred

sped

after Ed.

Ted saw

Ed's

red car

up ahead.

"Faster,

Fred!"

said Ted.

All of a sudden,

Ed stopped dead.

There was a roadblock

and a sign that read,

STOP! DO NOT DRIVE!

BIG CLIFF AHEAD!

"Fred!" called Ted.

"Stop the sled!"

But Fred

could not.

On they sped!

Ted and Fred

smashed into Ed.

Over

the

cliff

Ed

plumm-e-ted

along with

Ted

and

Fred.

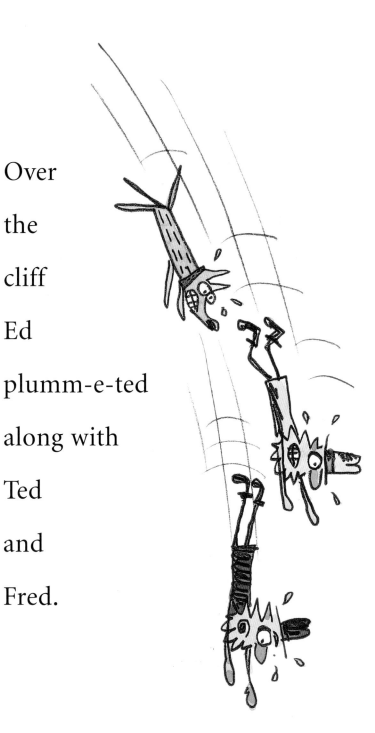

They

hit the water and

sank like lead.

Poor Ed

and Ted

and Ted's dog,

Fred!

They were

almost dead . . .

when they were swallowed

by a whale called Ned.

"Bother!" said Ed.

"Bother!" said Ted.

"Woof!" said Fred

as they bobbed around

in the belly of Ned.

But the whale called Ned—

who was overfed—

blew Ed

and Ted

and Fred

out of the hole

on the top

of his head.

Up,

up,

up,

flew

Ed

and

Ted

and

Fred

and

then . . .

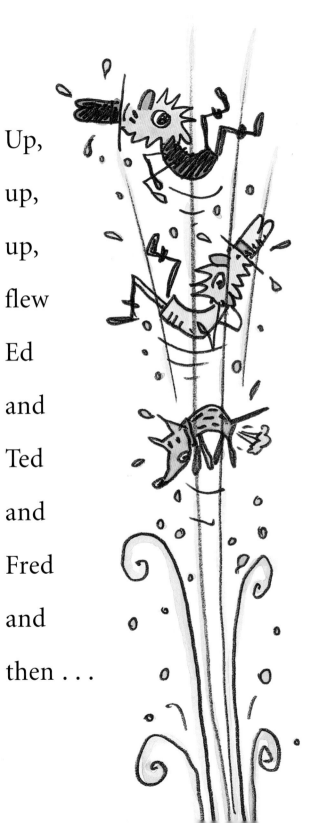

down,

down,

down,

they all did

head!

"Oh, no,"

said Ted.

"We'll end up

dead!"

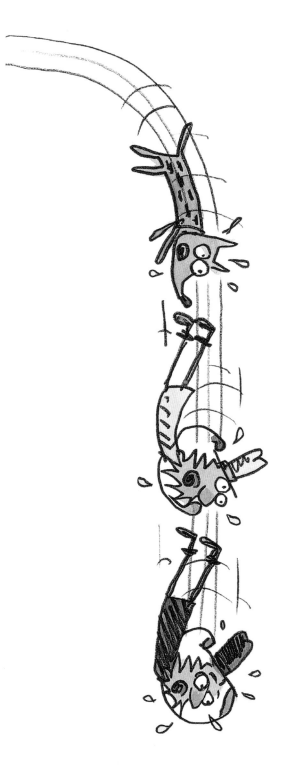

"Fear not,"

said Ed,

to his friend Ted,

stretching a

handkerchief

over his head.

"Hang on to me, Ted!

Hang on to Ted, Fred!"

And

down

to

the

ground

they

para-chu-ted.

"Thank you, Ed!"

said Ted.

"Thanks to you,

we are not dead!"

"Woof!" said Fred

as he jumped up

and licked

Ed's head.

Ed hugged Fred!

Fred hugged Ed!

Ted hugged Fred!

Fred hugged Ted!

 Ed hugged Ted!

Ted hugged Ed!

And

they

lived happily

ever after . . .

in their shed.